W9-ACR-296

DISCARD

Pete the Cat

Construction Destruction

Harperfestival is an imprint of HarperCollins Publishers.
Pete the Cat: Construction Destruction
www.harpercollinschildrens.com
Library of Congress catalog card number: 2014949449
ISBN 978-0-06-219861-7
14 15 16 17 18   SCP   10 9 8 7 6 5 4 3 2 1
❖
First Edition

"**R**ecess!" Pete shouts as the bell rings. But when Pete gets outside to play—oh no. The playground is a disaster. The swings are broken, the slide is rusty, and the sandbox is full of weeds.

Pete makes plans for a new playground.
"Wow!" says Principal Nancy. "Can you really build that?"
"Not by myself," says Pete. "I'm going to need some help."
"Whatever you need, Pete, it's yours."

The next day, Pete arrives at the playground before school. The construction crew is already there. He gives them the go-ahead to tear down the old playground.

Bang! Boom! Down goes the tower.

Honk! Honk! A truck arrives to recycle the metal.

The new playground equipment has arrived. It's time to get to work. The cement mixer will pour concrete. The dump truck will bring sand and dirt. The backhoe will dig. The whole team will get the job done.

Building a playground is hard work.

The new playground is cool, but it's not cool enough.
"What do you think?" Pete asks, holding up his latest plans.
"It will be too hard to build," says one of the workers.
"And everything is almost finished," says another.

"But it will make this the best playground ever," Pete says.
"Then let's do it," the workers say.

Screwdrivers twist in screws. Wrenches tighten the nuts. The workers try to make everything perfect.

Hooray!

The new playground is ready.

Everyone is disappointed—except for Pete.

This playground is filled with surprises and places to explore. The school playground is the most amazing playground ever.

Sometimes you've got to dare to dream big.